♀ □ ☽　　　　Diäteseong　　　9　8

☽ im ♉　　　　　　　　　　9　6

　　　　　　　　　　　　　9　3

naufgang 7 Uhr 15 M.　Untergang 4 Uhr 46

♄ □ ☽　　　　　　　　　9　1

☽ Erdn., ♂ □ □ ☽　　　8　58

6, 8 N.,　　　　　　　　8　55

　　　☿ ♄ ☽　　　　　8　53

　　　　　　　　　　　8　51

　　　　　　　　　　　8　48

♄ bei ☽　　　　　　　　8　46

nnenaufgang 7 Uhr 26 M.　Untergang 4 Uhr

　　　　　　　　extra　8　44

♃ u. ☍ bei ☽　　　　　8　42

7, 43 N.,　☿ in　　　　8　40

THE MORNING STAR

THE MORNING STAR

In Which the Extraordinary Correspondence of
Griffin & Sabine Is Illuminated

Written and Illustrated by
NICK BANTOCK

CHRONICLE BOOKS
SAN FRANCISCO

Library of Congress Cataloging-in-Publication Data available.

ISBN 0-8118-3199-X

Manufactured in China.

10 9 8 7 6 5 4 3 2 1

Book Design: Jacqueline Verkley / Byzantium Books Inc.

Chronicle Books LLC
85 Second Street
San Francisco, California 94105

www.chroniclebooks.com

To Holly

Somewhere in the sands of the desert...

Isabella—the Samoon has spoken and you should prepare to depart for Alexandria. However, before your hunger for Matthew can be satisfied there are certain precautions to be observed. Move fluidly by earth or water and stop to listen to the wind as it whispers your whereabouts. When I ran from Sabine and journeyed to the islands, the more I hurried across the sky, the more dislocated I became. By insulating myself from the elements, I failed my innate need to know exactly where I was. I would arrive, step into the landscape, and feel my body slip into confusion. A gentler pace will give you time to evolve. By keeping low to the ground you will also make yourself less conspicuous to Frolatti's dark angels. Savour the path and enjoy the sun. Griffin

Isabella de Reims
343, rue Maspero
Paris 75006
France

PAOLO 32

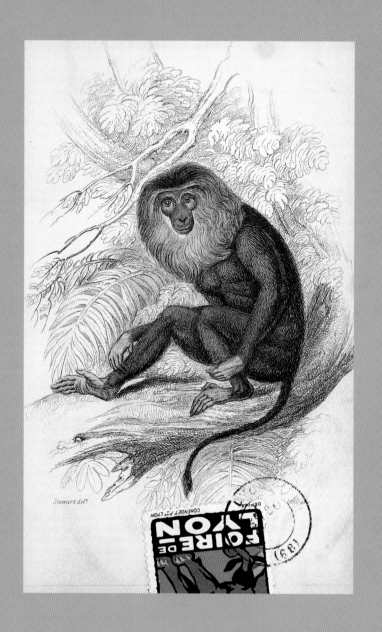

Stewart del.

COHENDET fils LYON

FOIRE DE LYON

(69)

Matthew

The longing to be with you was irresistible,
and as you can see, I'm already in Lyon. I
felt terrible about abandoning both
Prof. Lacourt and my thesis, but Griffin
strongly suggested that it was time to
leave Paris. He's arranged the finances
for my trip and has convinced me that I
should travel to Egypt in unhurried stages,
so it will be a few weeks before you can
expect me.
When I arrived here guess who
was casually sprawled out in my
hotel room? Minnaloushe!
How he got there I have no idea.
It's incredible that I missed the obvious. No
wonder he responds to the name Minnaloushe
— he is Griffin's cat!
In a few days I'll head to
Genoa where I can stay with
my cousin. You have her
address. Write to me there,
please.
I love you.

Isabella

Matthew Sedon
77 Sharea Otta
Alexandria
Egypt.

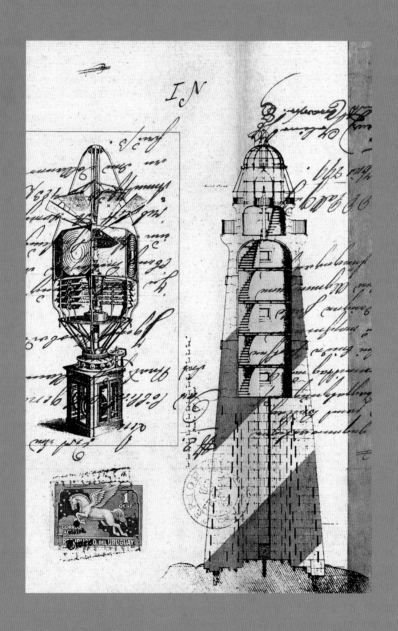

VICO CICALA 15
16126
GENOA
ITALY

ISABELLA de REIMS ℅ F. CONTI

Isabella
The other night during the storm, when I
sensed your departure, I felt such relief.
Now my nerves have grown tight again,
strung out by anticipation and frustration
that the dig continues to be out of bounds.
        The way you bellowed at Frolatti
when you found him sifting through the
papers in your room must have been something to behold. But I doubt he'll take
such a humiliating encounter lightly.
Promise me you'll keep up your guard. Who
knows who or what he really is and what he
wants from us.
        I have to admit I don't understand
why you can't come here immediately. But I
trust your instincts, so what can I say?
Would you consider it too romantic to think
of me as the Pharos Lighthouse guiding you
safely into port?
With all my love   Matthew

If Minnaloushe is Griffin's cat, wouldn't
that make him rather long in the whisker?

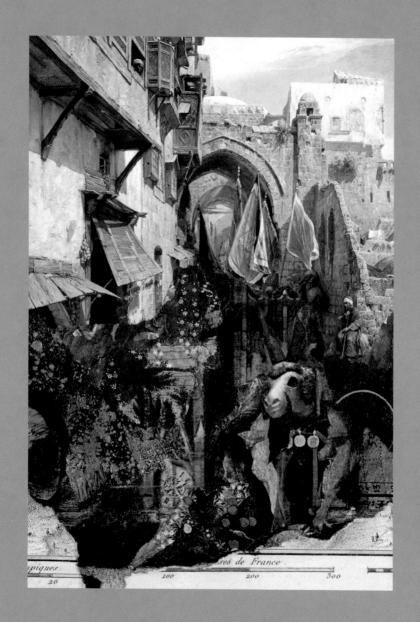

Sabine

I finally came to the conclusion that
Frolatti is going to ensure that the
site's closed down indefinitely and that
the only way I was going to get back in
was to do it in secrecy. I simply had to
see the sculpture again—I'm convinced
you're right when you say that it holds
some kind of compass or key.

Anyway, I waited till midnight
then slipped past the security guard
and into the chamber. After a thorough
but fruitless examination of the stone
(I really didn't have a clue what I was
looking for), I was about to leave, when
on impulse I switched off my torch and
ran my hand over the sculpture's schist
and alabaster surface. I immediately
detected something—the half of the sphere
that balanced on the baboon's head was
warm and smooth while the half above the
lion was icy and pitted with what felt
like tiny moonlike craters.

Given that you seem to understand
what's happening here, is there a chance
that you'll filter some insight to me?

J Matthew

SABINE STROHEM
39 LA PAZ PL.
SAN ROSA
PAOLO 9T6

Matthew — To imagine that we understand the reason behind everything that transpires would be a misconception, but our viewpoint certainly gives a different perspective. For example, we can tell you that in the darkness of the chamber, you touched the Morning Star. We can also surmise that Frolatti is exasperated by the elusiveness of his goal. He believes that Griffin and I have helped stir to the edge of waking a wisdom long buried in the sands. He thought the sculpture would point directly to that place of concealed knowledge, but he can find no clue within the figures to guide him. He suspects that, through me, you might be able to decipher that which is beyond him. You should do nothing. After all, you cannot reveal that which you do not know, can you? Sabine

Matthew Sedon
77 Sharea Offa
Alexandria
Egypt

PAOLO

Isabella

Sabine seems to want me to be passive,
but patience is something I've never
found very easy.

　　　Recently, I've been painting and
drawing a lot more. As much as I've
gained from seeing things through
Sabine's eyes, I think that unless I
impose more of myself on these pictures
I'll be in danger of disappearing into
her world. I have to take the skills
she's handed me and find a way of seeing
that's my own, separate from her
perceptions.

　　　Sensual images of you are forever
tangoing through my brain—maybe I can
begin solidify them. At least they would
be mine!

Love　Matthew

ISABELLA de REIMS
VICo CICALA 15
16126 GENoA
ITALY

PLATE 32

Griffin

    With the window flung open to the streets of Genoa I float in the lotus pond of my bedspread. A stone tablet rests across my belly, covered in flowers. Reaching to pluck a morsel, I'm enamoured to find that my fingers have narrowed into slender amber talons. I hook a blossom and lower it to my lips, marveling as a clover—sweet mustiness honeycombs across my tongue. Afterflavor shoots around my mouth and my whole body reverberates. I gulp down great mouthfuls of pond water that taste more exquisite than anything I could have imagined.

These sensations have continued beyond that waking dream. My mouth has developed an intelligence of its own—everything has savor, not just herbs and spices, but even this evening's pasta imparted to me the history of its birthplace in the wheat fields of Sicily. Isabella

Sabine

No dig to occupy me, and a lover in transit—I can see that my capacity to remain monumentally erect and inert is going to be tested to the full. Isn't there any way I can participate? Maybe distract Frolatti or something?

What exactly is this hidden wisdom he's hunting for? Does he believe that primary hermetic scrolls were removed from the great library before it was burnt? Or have I misread the tidbits of information you've been feeding me?

Another thing, the animal symbolism that we're coming up against keeps gnawing away at me. In Egyptian mythology, the sphinx and the gryphon were often interchangeable. If the lion is a constant in both creatures, wouldn't that also suggest man and falcon are interchangeable? An interesting concept!

Matthew

I thought the Morning Star was the planet Venus?

GPO

Isabella

There is a Renaissance proverb "Colei che si
lecca le labbra sa quale' il sapore della passione
del suo amante." ("She who licks her lips knows the taste
of her lover's desire.")

Your tongue has grown strong, your eyes have sharpened.
Soon all your senses will be like quicksilver.

As for Monsieur Minnaloushe, he was my Aunt Vereker's
cat. He watched over us and now probably considers
it his responsibility to keep a watchful eye on you. No
need to concern yourself with his well-being.
He's plenty able to fend for himself.

If you wanted to appeal to his
inexhaustible vanity, then I suggest
you occasionally ask him to dance.
        Griffin

PAOLO 32

LUFTPOST

Isabella de Reims
Vico Cicala 15
16126 Genoo
Italy

TUNISIE POSTES

Poste Aérienne 1f.

Matthew Sedon
Tshara Otta
Alexandra Egypt

Isabella de REIMS
ICTHOS HOTEL
MATALA
CRETE

Isabella

You're amazing. If it had been me, I'd have
probably taken to my heels. I can't get over
the fact that you were prepared to turn around
and challenge all four of them. What if they
had nothing to do with Frolatti, and were just
a bunch of men pursuing you because you were a
lone attractive woman?

     The stronger you grow the more I seem
to want you. You say you believe I'll respond
to your love—and I will. But now I understand
the self-doubts Griffin must have endured when
he knew he was to meet with Sabine. He was
troubled by the idea that he wouldn't be a
match for her soul. You and I are so like them.

Love   Matthew

DE SUEZ

POSTES

CANAL MARITIME

DE SUEZ

POSTES

PIROSCAFI
POSTALI
INTERNO

MATICU

RAL

S...LES

N AIR

NATIONA

FRANCE
ET
COLONIES } 2 fr. PAR
AN

ADRESSE

M. le Gérant du CHASSEUR FRANÇAIS
à SAINT-ÉTIENNE (Loire)

EGYPTE

TROUVÉE
OUVERTE
OU
DÉCHIRÉE
ET
RÉPARÉE
D'OFFICE.

ONE PIASTRE

POSTAGE

E.E.F.

E.E.F.

PAID

P° ëx Officio

Matthew Sedon
77 Sharea Otta
Alexandria
Egypt

7 584 1

ngo

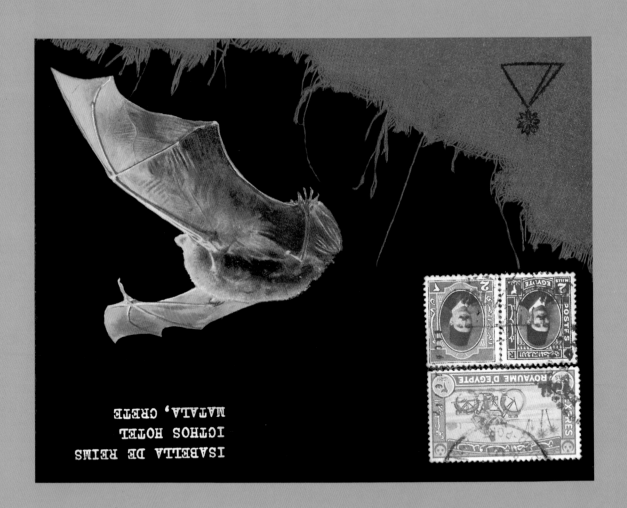

ISABELLA DE REIMS
ICTHOS HOTEL
MATALA, CRETE

Isabella — When I was a boy I used to go
to school atop a double-decker bus,
staring at the back-to-back houses and
their fogged bedroom windows. As each
eye-level pane flashed by I wondered
what dreams the inhabitants of those
rooms had witnessed the previous night.
I loved the idea of all those internal
worlds, separate and highly personal.
Then one day the possibility dawned on
me that our dreams were not separate
but joined. That maybe we do
not have dreams — dreams
have us. It frightened me, but a
truth rarely remains a threat
for long and eventually the
idea seemed to become almost
reassuring.
                    Griffin
the cat knows where it is
going. It carries you, and
you carry us.

Isabella de Reims
Icthos Hotel
Matala
Crete

Griffin

I am riding in
the neck fur of a cat
Either I am very small
or the cat is very large, for
the ground is far below me. We are loping through the ruins of Knossos.
When I look up I see a battalion of birds flying in from my left.
From my right comes another flock of similar magnitude.
Although they appear to be on collision course I am unprepared
for what is about to happen. The two armies smash headlong
into one another with a furious ear-splitting impact.
The Minoan sky is raining severed feathers. The grassy plain
has become thick with broken birds. But my cat carriage runs
on, paws skillfully high-stepping the pyres of fowl corpses.
We are relentless. Our destination awaits and it seems as
if nothing can hinder us.   Isabella

Correspondance

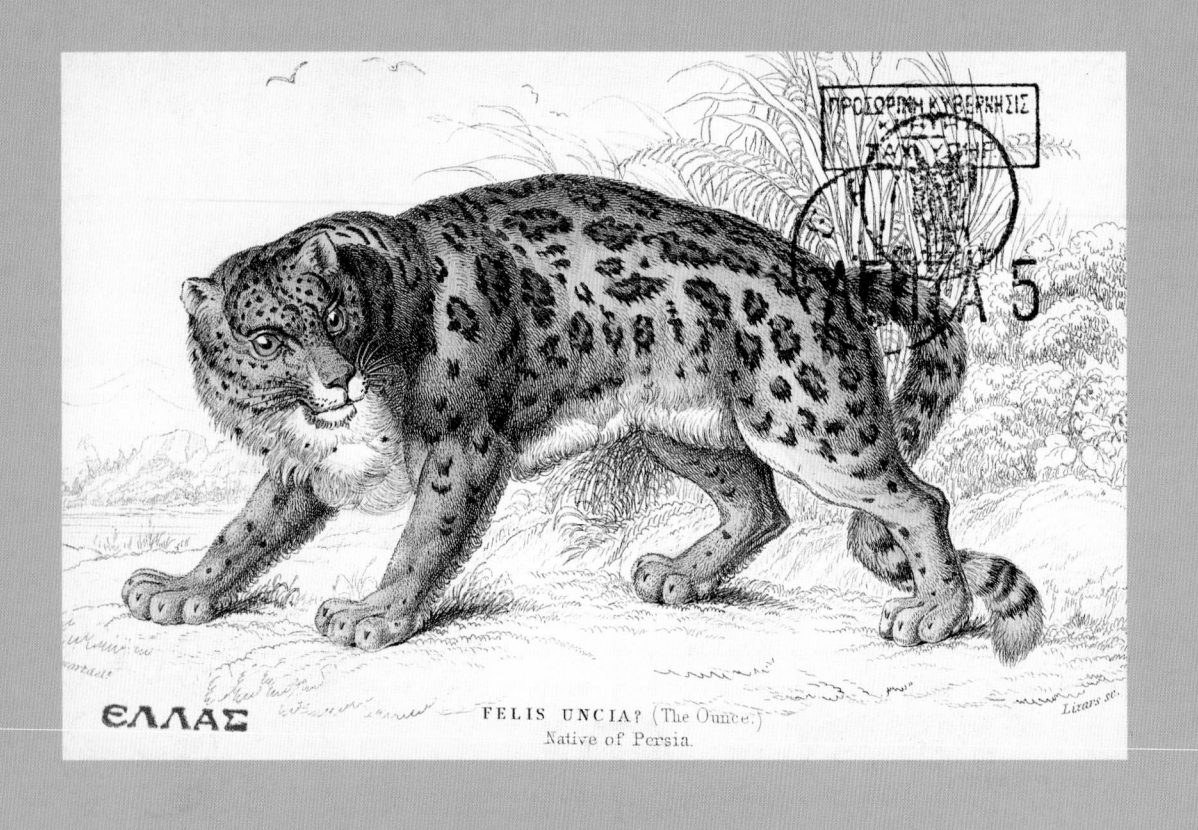

ΕΛΛΑΣ

FELIS UNCIA? (The Ounce.)
Native of Persia.

Lizars sc.

Sabine

Acting on your word, I drove out to a
place about 100 miles south of El Hammâm.
When I got there, I sank a hole and put
down a wire as if I was doing a sonar
test. Then I took lots of spurious
measurements, noting down the meaningless
figures very carefully. Finally, after
erecting a small magnetic beacon, I left
and returned to Alexandria.

     Assuming I was being watched by
Frolatti: he must really think I'm an
idiot. Or else he believes I've located
something of importance.

     I don't know if this charade has
achieved anything, but if nothing else
the illusion of action leaves me feeling
less like a goldfish swimming in glass
circles. *Matthew*

SABINE STROHEM
39 LA PAZ PL.
SAN ROSA
PAOLO 9T6

EGYPTE

Contains free

iverselle
arte. — Briefkaar
Postal.

Isabella
Unleash your wings and
fly swiftly as you are able
to Luxor. Frolatti has taken Matthew's
bait. He believes that he has prized
free the directions he seeks and that
this knowledge will allow him to prevent
the consummation of the sphinx. His
dark birds crisscross the desert sky,
searching the terrain for a glimpse
of the great cat. His resources are
far from limitless, and with his
attention cast upon the sands, you
may enter Egypt unimpeded.

Griffin

Isabella de Reims
Icthos Hotel
Matala
Crete

AIR MAIL

by ships catapult